ROCK·A·BYE
FARM

ROCK·A·BYE
FARM

by Diane Johnston Hamm

illustrated by Rick Brown

SIMON & SCHUSTER BOOKS FOR YOUNG READERS

Published by Simon & Schuster

New York ★ London ★ Toronto ★ Sydney ★ Tokyo ★ Singapore

SIMON & SCHUSTER BOOKS FOR YOUNG READERS
Simon & Schuster Building, Rockefeller Center
1230 Avenue of the Americas, New York, New York, 10020
Text copyright © 1992 by Diane Johnston Hamm. Illustrations copyright
© 1992 by Richard Brown. All rights reserved including the right of
reproduction in whole or in part in any form. SIMON & SCHUSTER
BOOKS FOR YOUNG READERS is a trademark of Simon & Schuster.
Designed by Lucille Chomowicz.
The text of this book is set in Breughel 55.
The illustrations were done in ink and watercolor.
Manufactured in México

Library of Congress Cataloging-in-Publication Data
Hamm, Diane Johnston. Rockabye farm / by Diane Hamm: illustrated by
Richard Brown. Summary: The Farmer helps his family and barnyard
animals fall asleep before drifting off himself. [1. Sleep—Fiction.]
I. Brown, Richard, 1941-   ill. II. Title. PZ7.H1837R63   1992
[E]—dc20   91-19127   ISBN 0-671-74773-8

For all who long to be rocked—DJH

To William Ross IV—RB

ROCK•A•BYE
FARM

It is bedtime.

The Farmer rocks his baby.

When the baby goes to sleep,

the Farmer rocks his dog.

When the dog is snoring loudly,

the Farmer rocks his hen.

When the hen has settled down,

the Farmer rocks his sheep.

When the sheep are dreaming well,

the Farmer rocks his pig.

When the pig no longer squeals,

the Farmer rocks his cow.

When the cow is tucked in straw,

the Farmer rocks his horse.

When the horse's eyelids close,

the Farmer rocks the mouse.

Now that everyone's asleep...

the Farmer rocks himself.

Good-Night.